Seemore the Seagull

Written by Ralph Tufo

Illustrated by Amanda Grafe

Photos of Revere Beach by Steve Levin

Leaning Rock Press

Leaning Rock Press
Gales Ferry, CT 06335
leaningrockpress@gmail.com
www.leaningrockpress.com

978-1-950323-54-8, Hardcover
978-1-950323-55-5, Softcover

Library of Congress Control Number: 2021910970

Publisher's Cataloging-In-Publication Data
(Prepared by The Donohue Group, Inc.)

Names: Tufo, Ralph, author. | Grafe, Amanda, illustrator. | Levin, Stephen J., photographer.
Title: Seemore the Seagull / written by Ralph Tufo ; illustrated by Amanda Grafe ;
    photos of Revere Beach by Stephen J. Levin.
Description: Gales Ferry, CT : Leaning Rock Press, [2021] | Interest age level: 004-010. |
    Summary: "Seemore the Seagull is a loveable people-watcher who observes the
    behavior of the diverse beach-goers on Revere Beach. He wants everyone to get along no
    matter what color, language, shape, or size. He becomes very upset when he sees some children
    argue and fight about sharing sand toys and destroying each other's sandcastles. He helps
    them learn to cooperate, and together they build a castle that makes them all happy"--Provided
    by publisher.
Identifiers: ISBN 9781950323548 (hardcover) | ISBN 9781950323555 (softcover)
Subjects: LCSH: Gulls--Juvenile fiction. | Cooperation--Juvenile fiction. | Sharing--Juvenile
    fiction. | Beachgoers--Juvenile fiction. | Revere Beach (Mass.)--Juvenile fiction. | CYAC:
    Gulls--Fiction. | Cooperation--Fiction. | Sharing--Fiction. | Beachgoers--Fiction. | Revere
    Beach (Mass.)--Fiction.
Classification: LCC PZ7.1.T84 Se 2021 | DDC [E]--dc23

Printed in the United States of America

This book is dedicated
to my wonderful family: Nancy, Steven, and David.
Thank you for always supporting me
in my many endeavors.

Seemore the Seagull
      loved to fly.
He'd flap his wings;
      take off to the sky.

Gliding, diving,
      catching a breeze,
Seemore the Seagull
      enjoyed being free.

He'd stretch his wings
    and soar up high;
Float among the clouds;
    zip through the sky.

He'd let a breeze take him,
    and cruise with the wind.
All the world below looked
    so beautiful to him.

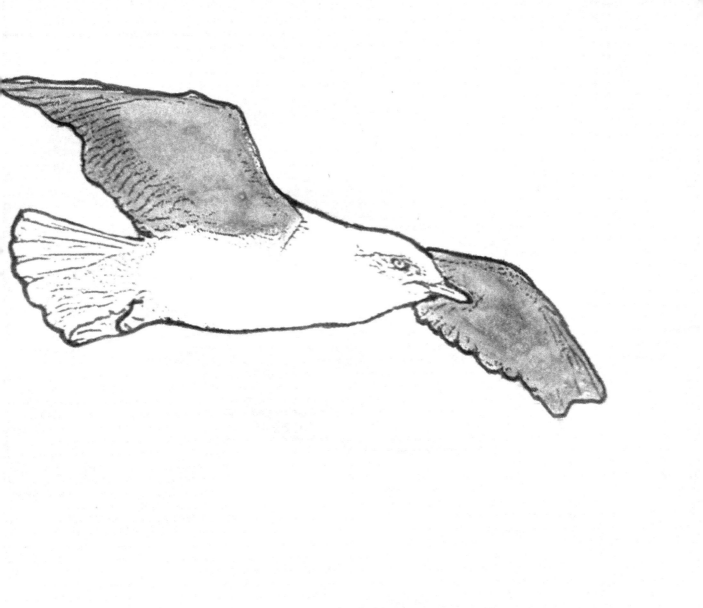

When he was hungry,
      he'd land on Revere Beach.
A feast of seafood
      was well within reach.

His favorite trash can
      was at Kelly's Roast Beef,
Filled with half-eaten dinners;
      what a seagull treat!

Sometimes he'd catch
    fried clams tossed his way.
It was a friendly game
    that children would play.

When he was extra hungry
    and just couldn't wait,
He'd snatch a sandwich
    off somebody's plate.

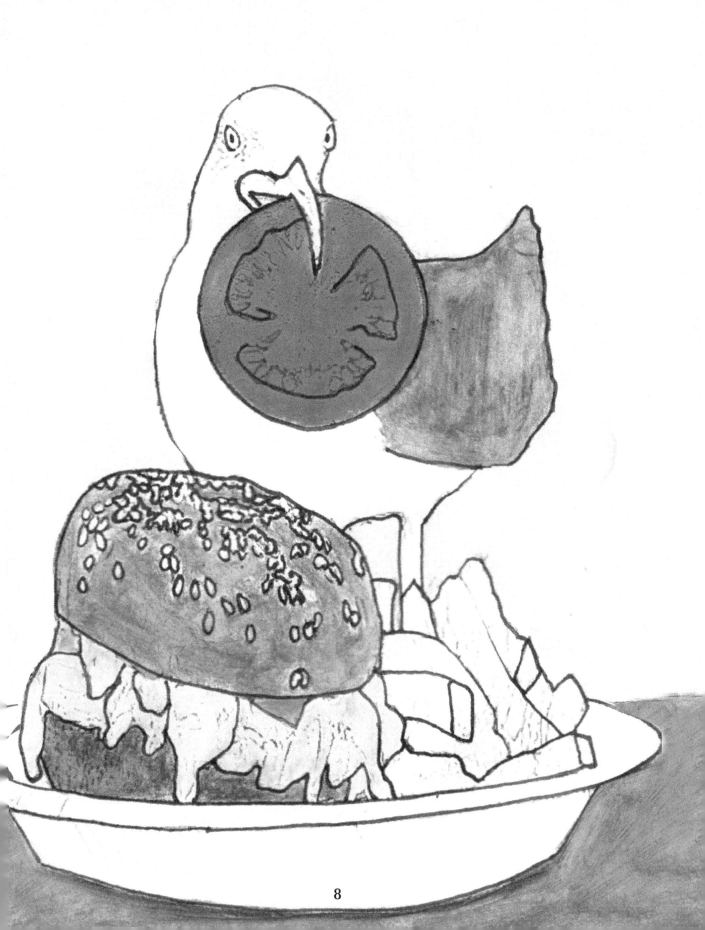

Perched on his look-out,
     he watched people pass by.
He loved all their different
     colors, shapes, and size.

Seemore could see more
     with his steady glare.
Nothing or no one escaped
     his bird's eye stare.

But something was bothering
    Seemore this day.
Why do some children seem
    to fight instead of play?

You knocked down my castle.
    You stole my pail.
But you splashed me first
    the other child wailed.

People are a puzzle, thought Seemore.
        They are an odd lot.
They think they're so different,
        but really they're not.

To me they all seem similar;
        they all act the same.
They're never wrong;
        someone else is to blame.

I see it all
        from my Revere Beach wall.
Why do some people refuse,
        to see things at all?

Even with binoculars,
        they can't see eye to eye.
When I see children fight,
        it really makes me cry.

I hear adults argue
        about stupid things.
Where they come from
        and the color of their skins.

I hear them complain
        how others talk.
But we seagulls just laugh together,
        Awk, Awk, Awk.

I see children quarrel,
    scream, and fight.
I wish they'd all stop
    trying to be right.

At my beach,
    I want all to get along,
So I'll help these children
    learn right from wrong.

With Seemore's help,
     they built a most wonderful sight.
They learned to cooperate
     rather than fight.

They built a sand castle,
     sturdy and tall.
It made the children
     both happy after all.

One dug water canals;
     the other piled sand.
They gave each other
     a helping hand.

Building a castle together
     was much more fun.
By learning to share,
     they both had won.

Seemore the Seagull
    began to get sleepy.
After all, people-watching
    isn't that easy.

So Seemore the Seagull
    flew off home to sleep.
A quiet, cozy spot nestled
    on the beach.

He'll hear the ocean waves;
     sleep beneath the moon beams.
Visions of fries and clams
     will light up his dreams.

And maybe just maybe,
      he'll dream of a morning tide,
That will sweep away
      all the fears that we hide.

Author

Ralph Tufo is a retired college professor and has been a professional musician for over 35 years. His band, **The Squeezebox Stompers**, tours throughout New England. He has released 11 CD recordings and has received four Boston Music Awards.

In addition to writing *Seemore the Seagull*, he has written several short plays, over 50 songs, and 3 full-length musicals. *The Katrina Roadhouse* musical is about the aftermath of Hurricane Katrina. The musical comedy, *I'd Rather Be Lucky Than Good,* is about golf, fate, and friendship, and *Beyond the Blues* is a Zoom Production recorded in 2021 about the power of music in overcoming life's difficulties. A live production of *Beyond the Blues* is scheduled for production in the Spring of 2022.

Ralph's had several staged readings of plays at the following venues: North Shore Community College, Internal Matter in South Boston, and the Community Church of Boston. His play, *Wrong Place, Right Time,* was produced at the Boston Playwright's Platform Festival and the Saugus Theater Company's Staged Readings.

To view **The Squeezebox Stompers'** video of the sea chantey, *Seemore the Seagull*, along with other related information, log on to www.squeezeboxstompers.com and click on the "Sea Chantey" tab at the top of the website.

Contact Ralph if you'd like a book reading or a performance of the sea shanty, "*Seemore the Seagull*" at: ralphtufo@gmail.com

The Squeezebox Stompers

Illustrator

Amanda Grafe is an author and illustrator from New England. She enjoys spending time with her dog, writing about the arts, and making the world a better place. In addition to illustrating the books in Julia Reid's **Alex and the Magical Coat Series**, Amanda has authored three of her own children's books, **My Best Ghoul Friend, Baby Bunny and the Balloon,** and **The Sneaky Mouse**, illustrating two of them.

Photographer

Steve Levin spent his childhood in Chelsea, MA and neighboring Revere Beach was always a favorite destination. Today it remains his favorite place to visit or take long walks with his dog, Bella, who loves and appreciates the long crescent shape of this first public beach as much as Steve does.

Steve's interest in art began in grade school when, at age 9, his collage was chosen for an exhibit at the Public Library. That interest continued through his student and adult life.

Recently his work has been exhibited in several galleries in Boston and the North Shore. Steve's Professional affiliations include the Griffin Museum of Photography, Lynn Arts Association, ReachArts Swampscott, Greater Lynn Photography Association, Newburyport Arts Association, and Marblehead Arts Association. All photos are copyrighted.

To contact Steve:
email him at: stephenjlevin@gmail.com or visit his website at: https://stephenjlevin.com/

Photos of Revere Beach

In 1896, Revere Beach became the first public beach in the country. With its three-mile crescent-shaped sandy beach, it soon became a favorite of beach-goers throughout New England. Its history includes an exciting amusement park with rides like the world-famous Cyclone roller coaster. Dance ballrooms, arcades, and restaurants added to the family-friendly atmosphere of the beach. With easy access by public transportation or by car, the beach has a history of attracting a diverse population of people from the city or the suburbs. Today, Revere beach is noted for its Kite Flying Festival and International Sand Sculpting Festival, attracting people from all over the world.

With "Photo-Painting" Steve combines the art of photography with the art of painting, aways respecting the original subject. He creates an image, using available technology, that has the qualities of both photography and painting.

CPSIA information can be obtained
at www.ICGtesting.com
Printed in the USA
BVHW062131220821
614828BV00003B/49